Dear Reader,

This book is completely by me, I did all the words and all the pictures and it took me ages. It's about all the strange things that get me into trouble. Strange things that are SO STRANGE no one EVER believes me.

When I try telling grown-ups what REALLY happened they shake their heads and say: 'DON'T MAKE UP STORIES OR YOUR NOSE WILL GROW LONG!' But I'm not making up stories. Everything I'm about to tell you is true. It all REALLY HAPPENED!

signed Jake Cake

Michael Broad spent much of his childhood gazing out of the window imagining he was somewhere more interesting.

Now he's a grown-up Michael still spends a lot of time gazing out of the window imagining he's somewhere more interesting – but now he writes and illustrates books as well.

Some of them are picture books, like *Broken Bird* and *The Little Star Who Wished*.

Books by Michael Broad

JAKE CAKE AND THE ROBOT DINNER LADY
JAKE CAKE AND THE WEREWOLF TEACHER

JAKE CAKE

THE WEREWOLF TEACHER

MICHAEL BROAD

PUFFIN

This book is dedicated to my friend John

PUFFIN BOOKS

Published by the Penguin Group
Penguin Books Ltd, 80 Strand, London WC2R 0RL, England
Penguin Group (USA) Inc., 375 Hudson Street, New York, New York 10014, USA
Penguin Group (Canada), 90 Eglinton Avenue East, Suite 700, Toronto, Ontario, Canada M4P 2Y3
(a division of Pearson Penguin Canada Inc.)
Penguin Ireland, 25 St Stephen's Green, Dublin 2, Ireland (a division of Penguin Books Ltd)
Penguin Group (Australia), 250 Camberwell Road, Camberwell, Victoria 3124, Australia
(a division of Pearson Australia Group Pty Ltd)
Penguin Books India Pvt Ltd, 11 Community Centre, Panchsheel Park, New Delhi – 110 017, India
Penguin Group (NZ), 67 Apollo Drive, Mairangi Bay, Auckland 1310, New Zealand
(a division of Pearson New Zealand Ltd)
Penguin Books (South Africa) (Pty) Ltd, 24 Sturdee Avenue, Rosebank, Johannesburg 2196, South Africa

Penguin Books Ltd, Registered Offices: 80 Strand, London WC2R 0RL, England

penguin.com

Published 2007
1

Copyright © Michael Broad, 2007
All rights reserved

The moral right of the author has been asserted

Set in Perpetua by Palimpsest Book Production Limited,
Polmont, Stirlingshire
Made and printed in England by Clays Ltd, St Ives plc

British Library Cataloguing in Publication Data
A CIP catalogue record for this book is available from the British Library

ISBN: 978–0–141–32087–8

Here are three UNBELIEVABLE stories about the times I met:

JAKE CAKE
AND THE
WEREWOLF TEACHER

The trouble started when I fell asleep in Mrs Beady's maths class, which to begin with wasn't completely my fault because maths is really boring and if it was more interesting I probably would've stayed awake.

I was having a very nice dream about *not* being in a maths class when Mrs Beady prodded me with her special 'prodding' ruler and I nearly fell off my chair.

'Are we keeping you awake, Mr Cake?' she said, and sang it like a rhyme, which was even worse because the rest of the class started giggling. Everyone always makes fun of my name. They call me Carrot Cake, Jaffa Cake, Cup Cake and just about any other kind of cake you can think of. My mum even calls me Angel Cake! She thinks it's cute, but it's just really embarrassing. Mrs Beady was looming over me and I didn't know what to say because everyone was watching, so I said, 'I wasn't asleep, I was just resting my eyelids.' Which is something my dad says when he falls asleep in front of the TV.

The other kids started laughing but Mrs Beady didn't even crack a smile. I don't think she has a very good sense of humour, which is probably because she's a maths teacher. I know if I was a maths teacher I wouldn't smile either.

Mrs Beady was cross and made me stay behind

bored

after school to write 'I must not fall asleep in class when I could be learning lots of wonderful things' one hundred times! And when I started writing 'I must not fall asleep in class when I could be learning lots of wonderful things' Mrs Beady had the cheek to FALL ASLEEP at her desk!

I'm not the fastest writer
in the whole wide
world so by the time I
finished it was
already getting
dark outside and
my teacher was
snoring like a

prodding

ruler

tractor. I crept up to her desk and
prodded Mrs Beady with her special
'prodding' ruler.

She snuffled awake and nearly fell
off her chair, which is only fair
because that's how I felt when she
prodded me.

'Finished!' I said cheerily before she
could realize what had happened.

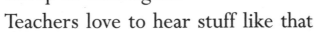

Mrs Beady ignored the pages I was
waving and started looking around
in a panic.

'What time is it?' she gasped.

I said it was 5 p.m., and that 5 p.m.
is very late for a kid to still be at

school, especially
in winter when it
gets dark so early.
I also said I'd
definitely learned
my lesson and
would never ever fall
asleep in class again.

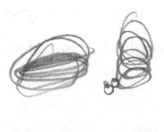

Teachers love to hear stuff like that

because it makes them think they're in charge, even when they're not.

But Mrs Beady wasn't listening. She was staring at the open diary on her desk. Across the page were the words

'GET HOME BEFORE SUNSET AND BUY LOTS OF RAW STEAK!' scribbled in big red letters.

Mrs Beady looked out of the window at the big full moon shining in the sky. Her eyes grew very wide and then she started scratching behind her ear the way dogs do when they have fleas.

FULL MOON

NOT A FULL MOON

I was trying to remember whether
Mrs Beady's eyes had always been
bright yellow when, quick as a flash,
she jumped up from her seat and
shooed me towards the door with my
coat and scarf.

'Off you go then! Well done! Don't
do it again!' she trilled.

Mrs Beady seemed in a
really big hurry to get
rid of me, which was
fine by me. I didn't
want to hang around
in school any
longer than I
needed to.

I put on my coat and scarf and was just about to leave when I realized I was still holding the hundred lines that Mrs Beady hadn't even bothered to look at. I turned round – just in time to see my teacher disappear into the art cupboard. She slammed the door behind her and lots of banging and clanging and crashing started coming from inside.

Something weird was definitely going on.

I told myself I needed to hand over my lines, but really I was being nosy and wanted to know what my maths teacher was up to.

'Is everything OK, Mrs Beady?' I called, knocking on the cupboard door.

The banging and
clanging and crashing
stopped and Mrs Beady made a loud
grunting sound, which to be honest
could have been a 'yes' *or* a 'no'.

'Do you want to check my lines
before I go home?' I added, listening
carefully with my ear against the door.

Mrs Beady was silent for a moment and
then said, 'OoooooooowwwwwwW!' in a
very loud voice, which I took to mean,
'Yes, dear boy, I would love to
see the hundred lines you
worked so hard on.'

So I took a deep breath
and opened the
art-cupboard door.

At first I thought Mrs Beady
had been eaten by a GREAT
BIG WOLF! Until I
noticed the GREAT
BIG WOLF was wearing Mrs Beady's
dress and glasses and shoes.

In *Little Red Riding Hood* the wolf went around wearing a nightdress and bonnet after eating the girl's granny, but that's just a story. This was so much stranger because it was real, and I needed to work out what was going on. And I needed to work it out fast because the GREAT BIG WOLF was staring right at me with its big yellow eyes.

'Mrs Beady, you've turned into a WOLF!' I said, having put two and two together, which I suppose is maths,

so Mrs Beady would have been
very pleased if she were not
already busy being a great big
werewolf.

My maths teacher was a
GREAT BIG WEREWOLF!

Mrs Beady snatched the pages
from my hand, chewed them up

with her big wolf teeth, swallowed
them and then dribbled all over my
shoes. She grinned at me in a
mischievous wolfy way and then leapt
over my head and bolted through the
classroom door.

At this point you would probably expect me to run screaming all the way home (and it was tempting because I was a bit scared), but I'd never seen a werewolf before and I wanted to see what it was going to do next.

So I ran after Mrs Beady.

It was easy to see where she'd gone because there was a trail of frothy drool all along the corridor. But it was pretty spooky because everyone had gone home and the school was completely empty. When I finally caught up with Mrs Beady she was in the canteen.

The whole place looked like it had been turned upside down and Mrs Beady was in the middle of the room eating cold burgers and cold chips and cold 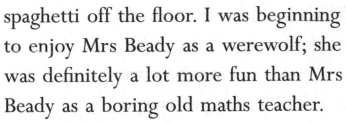 spaghetti off the floor. I was beginning to enjoy Mrs Beady as a werewolf; she was definitely a lot more fun than Mrs Beady as a boring old maths teacher.

So I decided to keep her.

While she was busy licking the floor with her big wolf tongue I tied my scarf round her furry neck to use as a lead.

'You're coming home with me, OK, Mrs Beady?' I said, pulling the stubborn animal away from the food and back down the corridor. She didn't want to leave the burgers behind so I had to drag my maths teacher most of the way with her bottom sliding along the polished wooden floors.

When we eventually got outside Mrs Beady started acting up and became a bit difficult to manage. She kept chasing the wheels of cars and buses and bicycles. In fact she tried

to chase anything that moved and it took all of my strength to stop her getting away. I had to pull her all the way down the high street and all the time she kept jumping up at people, trying to lick them on the face and eat their shopping – which definitely isn't proper behaviour for a teacher.

There were lots of screams from passers-by, and this was a lot of fun because EVERYONE got out of our way.

I even saw some kids from school
who said my new dog was the coolest
thing they'd ever seen and stopped
to pet her. They hugged her neck

and scratched
her head and
rubbed her
belly. It made
me laugh to
imagine what
they would say if they knew
it was old Mrs Beady they were
making such a fuss over!

When we eventually got
home Mum and Dad were
watching TV in the
living room, so I
took Mrs Beady
in to meet
them.

'What on earth are you doing with
that great big ugly dog!' Mum
screamed, lifting her legs
up in case Mrs Beady
might want to gnaw on her ankles.
'This is Mrs Beady,' I said. 'She's turned
into a werewolf. Can I keep her?'

'I've told you before about bringing stray dogs home. Now get rid of that ugly brute this instant!' Mum said, looking very angry. Mrs Beady made a low rumbling growl and Mum quickly sat back in her chair.

'It's not a stray dog,' I pleaded. 'It really is Mrs Beady. She turned into a werewolf in the art cupboard at school! Honestly!'

'How many times do I have to tell you,' said Mum. 'DON'T MAKE UP STORIES OR YOUR NOSE WILL GROW LONG!'

'But, Mum . . .'

'You heard your mother,' said Dad. Although he didn't look up so he may

have been resting his eyelids. Dad
doesn't usually get involved in family
arguments. He just agrees with Mum
when she gives him a look, and Mum
was definitely giving him a look.

I knew the discussion
was over and that I was
in big trouble, but I
couldn't send Mrs Beady

mum giving
a Look,
SCARY!

out into the cold dark night all on
her own. So I sneaked her up to my
room.

Sneaking a GREAT BIG WEREWOLF
up to your room is much more difficult
than it sounds. It involved lots of
shoving and nudging and growling –
until two yellow wolf eyes set their
sights on our cat Fatty who was
dozing at the top of the
stairs.

Fatty hissed and
puffed up like a
giant pompom
when he saw
my new pet.

Then he
scarpered,
quickly
followed by
Mrs Beady who
took off like a
rocket, dragging
me behind her.

Bump
Bump
Bump

I bumped up every stair
along the way and all I could
think was that Mum would *definitely*
come to investigate all the racket.

Fatty managed to escape into one of
his hiding places, leaving a very
confused werewolf behind. And while
she was busy trying to work it out I
bundled Mrs Beady into my room.

There aren't many places to hide a GREAT BIG WEREWOLF in my room, but when I heard Mum running up the stairs after me I had to think fast, so I shoved Mrs Beady into the wardrobe.

Mum came in and gave me a stern talking-to about making so much noise and bringing stray dogs home and making up silly stories that aren't true.

I kept quiet
and hoped Mrs
Beady would do
the same until Mum
went back
downstairs.
Suddenly the
wardrobe door
creaked open and
I could see Mrs Beady
grinning at me with a pair of my
pants on her head. She looked so
funny it made me laugh.

Mum didn't look
round to see the big-
grinning-wolf-with-
pants-on-its-head.

mum looking
Angry!

ooooOWWW!

Instead she got very annoyed
at my laughing and said I
would have to stay in my
room until I could take
things seriously.

It's a good thing Mum left
when she did, because that's
when the HOWLING
started!

But it wasn't Mrs Beady
howling, although she did seem quite
excited. It was coming from the
garden. I looked out of the
window and saw yet *another*
werewolf sitting on the
lawn, and this one was
even bigger than my one.

For a moment I considered swapping them over, or even having two werewolves, but I decided it wouldn't be fair on Mrs Beady. Besides, she was already becoming a bit too much of a handful.

'Sorry, we already have a werewolf here, thank you,' I said, and was about to close the window when the werewolf answered back!

'Is your werewolf's name Agatha Beady by any chance?' he said in a very polite voice. Before I could answer, Mrs Beady sprang from her hiding place, bringing the whole contents of the wardrobe with her. 'Is that you, George?' she called out, rolling around in the pile of clothes. 'That's my husband, George,' she said, grinning up at me with her big wolf teeth.

I don't know if I was more surprised that Mrs Beady the werewolf could talk, or that the other werewolf had jumped from the garden and into my room in one huge leap, landing none too gently on the carpet.

It was then that something really
horrible happened. Something so
horrible and terrible I find it difficult
to write down the words.

Mr and Mrs Beady started
SNIFFING BOTTOMS!!!

'EXCUSE ME!' I shouted, covering
my eyes. 'WOULD YOU MIND
NOT SNIFFING BOTTOMS IN
MY ROOM, PLEASE!' They did seem

very happy to see each other though. It was actually quite romantic, in a werewolfy kind of way.

I was wondering to myself if I could somehow keep them both when I heard Mum's heavy footsteps charging up the stairs again and I panicked. The werewolves heard it too because they stopped sniffing bottoms and their ears pricked up.

'I think it's time to go, dear,' said Mr Beady, nodding goodbye to me before jumping back through the window into the night.

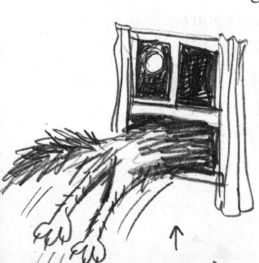

mr Beady

Mrs Beady
leapt after him
and paused at the
window sill.

mrs Beady

'Goodbye, Jake Cake, and
thank you for the hundred lines. They
really were rather delicious!' she said,
licking her lips. And then Mrs Beady
was gone too.

I was left with no werewolves, no
explanation for all the commotion or
for the great big mess
in my room,
and a very
angry Mum
who wanted
answers.

But I wasn't going to risk
telling the truth again.

Mum made me go to bed early that
night, after tidying my room and
promising not to bring any more stray
dogs home, or make up stories that
aren't true.

As Mum closed my window an eerie
HOWLING could be heard in the
distance. She looked up at the full
moon and then eyed me suspiciously.
She paused for a moment, frowned,
then she quickly drew the curtains and
went downstairs.

OOOoooOWWWWW!

FULL MOON
Again

39

Mrs Beady wasn't at school the next day so we had a supply teacher instead. I made sure I stayed awake during her class, because Mrs Beady's replacement REALLY looked like trouble!

JC

Jake Cake
Productions

JAKE CAKE

AND THE

MONSTER

Babysitter

Every time Mum and Dad go out together I *always* get a big long lecture about behaving myself for the babysitter.

'. . . and when we get home I don't want to hear any made-up stories

about grannies from outer space
or any other such nonsense,' Mum
said, eyeing me fiercely as she pulled
on her coat.

'Yes, Mum,' I said, even though
I didn't make up the granny from
outer space. She was real, but I'll tell
you about her another time.

'. . . because you know what will happen if you make up stories, don't you?' she added sternly.

'My nose will grow long,' I mumbled.

'Exactly!' she said as the doorbell rang.

The new babysitter was a tall, clumsy girl with pigtails and glasses. She struggled through the door with a huge pile of books and a big, heavy schoolbag.

'Hello, Mrs Cake,' she panted.

'Hello, Sally,' Mum said, frowning at the bag. 'Are you moving in with us?'

'Oh, this is just my homework,' Sally laughed. 'I thought I would study when Jake goes to bed. I hope that's OK?'

'Of course, dear,' Mum said. 'It's always good to see young people keen on their schoolwork.' She nodded in my direction and added, 'This one's *not* so keen on his schoolwork, unfortunately.'

Sally looked down at me with a friendly smile as if to say, *I'm your new*

*babysitter and we're going to get along
great!* But I wasn't taken in. Every
kid knows you can't judge a
babysitter until your parents have left
the house. That's when you *really* find
out what you're up against. But at
least Sally was young. The old ones
always try to get you in bed early so
they can watch all their soap operas
on TV.

Dad's horn sounded in the driveway,
meaning it was time to leave, and
Mum got all in a fluster. 'Now, my
mobile number is above the phone so
if you have any trouble just give me a
call,' she said to the
babysitter.

'Yes, Mrs Cake.' Sally
nodded responsibly.
'Now behave
yourself for Sally,
Angel Cake,' Mum
added, kissing my cheek
and leaving a big smudge of
lipstick behind. I rubbed my cheek as
she hurried out to the car and we both
waved as they drove away.

'Angel Cake?' Sally chuckled as
she closed the door.

I shrugged as if
to say, *Don't
ask!*

I've had a lot
of trouble with

Sally and me waving

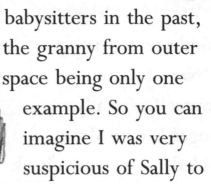

babysitters in the past, the granny from outer space being only one example. So you can imagine I was very suspicious of Sally to begin with. But she seemed very nice and normal and even let me have crisps and biscuits while watching *my* programmes on TV. So eventually I stopped worrying and settled down for a quiet evening.

my beanbag

'What's that?' I asked as Sally
arranged all her books on the table and
pulled a great big jar of brown goo
from inside her bag.

'It's my science project from school,'
she said, turning the jar and studying
its contents. 'I have to hand it in to my
teacher tomorrow. I've been working

on the formula for weeks now
and I think it's almost
finished.'

'What's it meant to be?' I asked,
gazing through the glass as the gloopy
brown liquid churned and bubbled like
volcano lava.

'Runny Chocolate!'
she declared excitedly.
'It's a brand-new kind
of chocolate that I
invented all by
myself.'

'What's different
about it?' I asked.

'Well,' said Sally. 'Like
the name says, it's *runny*.

Runny
Chocolate!

It doesn't set hard like
normal chocolate, which
means you can eat it with a spoon,
drink it with a straw, or just dip your
hand in and then lick it all off.'

'Wow!' I said. 'Can I try some?'

'When it's finished. But first I have to
add the secret
ingredient,' Sally
said, glancing at her
watch. 'And I'm
afraid it's already
past your
bedtime.'

I grumbled as
Sally sent me off to bed, but
decided it wouldn't be a good idea to

give the-babysitter-who-could-make-chocolate any trouble. I knew when I was on to a good thing.

But as I lay in bed I couldn't help wondering what was going on downstairs and whether Sally had added the secret ingredient. After five minutes of tossing and turning I decided to sneak down and see how she was doing.

Peeping through the banisters I saw my babysitter flicking through her science books, mixing different ingredients into the jar and scribbling things down in her notebook. She had big plastic goggles on over her glasses and looked just like a mad professor.

Sally stirred up the jar with a big wooden spoon and occasionally lifted it out to sniff the bubbling goo. Each time she added something new and then stirred the whole thing up again. This went on for quite a while until eventually she reached inside her bag and carefully pulled out a smaller jar.

The secret ingredient! I thought.

Sally held the small jar up to her face and the amber liquid inside seemed to glow. 'Honey to make the Runny!' she

 said to herself, and then slowly poured it into the bigger jar.

Sally stirred the
concoction three times,
set the spoon down,
closed the notebook and
took a long deep
breath. She eyed the
jar carefully, dipped
her finger inside, twirled it
around and scooped out a big fat
blob of Runny Chocolate.
I held my breath as she
popped it in her mouth.
Sally concentrated as she absorbed all
the flavours and her frown slowly
turned into a smile. She helped herself
to another scoop and her smile grew
into the biggest grin I've ever seen.

She's done it! I thought. *My very own babysitter has invented a brand-new kind of chocolate!*

I had to get a closer look! My plan was to ask for a glass of water as though I'd been asleep and just happened to wander downstairs. I've donc it loads of times with babysitters and they always fall for it. But as I approached, yawning and rubbing the pretend sleep from my eyes, Sally's belly made a very unusual sound that stopped me in my tracks.

Boing, boing, boing, it went, like a distant bongo drum.

59

I completely forgot
my excuse for being
out of bed and stared
at Sally as her belly-
drum grew louder
and louder,
grumbling and
groaning like
rocks in a washing machine. Sally
stared back at me with a very worried
look on her face,

oops!

Sally's worried
LOOK

and then burped like a foghorn before disappearing under the table.

Sally burped and belched and blew off like a set of windy bagpipes. The table shook, the tablecloth billowed out and the jar of Runny Chocolate rocked backwards and forwards, slopping all over the place.

I froze to the spot, not knowing what to do, when the table suddenly stopped moving and everything went scarily quiet.

GULP!

I lifted the corner of the tablecloth.

'Sally?' I whispered, peering nervously underneath. 'Are you OK?'

But Sally was gone. All that remained was a pair of plastic goggles and the stinky smell of rotten sprouts. I scratched my head and wondered what could have happened. Had she evaporated? Disappeared into thin air? Did the Runny Chocolate make her shrink or turn invisible?

Mum gets cross when I lose a library

book, or a sock, or even a button off my shirt. So I could just imagine how much trouble I'd be in if she thought I'd lost a whole babysitter!

Then I heard something strange behind me, something burping and belching loudly with smelly sprouty breath and a tumbling, grumbling stomach. I knew it had to be Sally, but the shadow cast over me was a whole lot bigger than it should have been.

I turned round slowly to find Sally
standing over me. She was now
roughly twice the size she had been.
Her massive shoulders were hunched
forward and great heavy arms dangled

at her sides. Her large mouth was full
of crooked yellow teeth and she was
dribbling all down her chin.

In fact the only way I even knew the
monster was Sally was because she was
still wearing pigtails and glasses.

The Sally Monster looked very
confused, and as I smiled helplessly
up at her she furrowed her
massive bushy brows and grunted.

Then she leaned
forward and
sniffed my hair
as if trying to
work out whether
I was food
or not.

sniff

65

The Monster *was* Sally my babysitter, but it was obvious the Sally Monster had no idea who or what *I* was, and if I didn't do something quickly I could end up being dinner.

ARRRRGGGGHHH!!

'ARRRRRRRGGGGHHHHHH!' I screamed at the very top of my voice. Which, by the way, is the only sensible thing to do when confronted with a monster, especially a big, stupid one who doesn't know the difference between people and food.

The Sally Monster was frightened by
the noise. She clasped her huge hands
over her ears and began running
around the room in a panic, crashing
into and crushing everything that got
in her way.

It seemed the
Sally Monster
was more
afraid of me
than I was of
her, so I had
to try to calm
her down before
she wrecked the
whole house. But
when I tried to
approach, she leapt up on to the light
fitting and dangled there, shaking like
a leaf.

The monster peered down at me the
way a frightened elephant looks down
at a mouse.

'It's OK,' I said in my most soothing voice. 'I won't hurt you.'

The Sally Monster frowned at me again and I actually felt sorry for her.

'Come down, it's OK,' I said. Her eyes widened a bit as though she was beginning to trust me, and, after a few more minutes of coaxing, she eventually jumped down.

Holding her big heavy hand I led the giant, bumbling Sally Monster to the sofa and sat her down. 'There, there,' I said, patting her hand. 'There's a good monster.'

Sally was just beginning to calm
down when our cat Fatty leapt up on
the arm of the sofa and set her off
again. The Sally Monster screamed
and hid behind her pigtails as Fatty
sauntered casually along the back of
the sofa.

Fatty didn't show the slightest interest in the Sally Monster. He had his eyes on something far more interesting.

The fat cat leapt from the corner of the sofa and on to the table with a thud, which was the most energetic thing I've ever seen him do. Being the laziest, greediest cat in the world there was only one thing he could be after. The jar of Runny Chocolate!

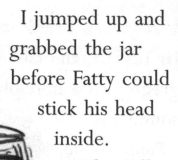 I jumped up and
grabbed the jar
before Fatty could
stick his head
inside.

The Sally
Monster was
still hiding
behind her
pigtails so I
decided to get rid of the
strange brown goo once and for all
before it could do any more damage.

I took the jar into the
bathroom and flushed its
contents down the loo.
Phew! No more monsters for me!

But when I took the empty
jar back to the table I was
greeted by a horribly familiar
sound.

Boing, *boing*, *boing*, it went,
like a very distant bongo
drum.

I looked down and Fatty
was staring up at me with
a very strange look on his face.
The cat had Runny Chocolate
stuck to his whiskers and all
round him there were
sticky brown paw prints
across the pages of Sally's
books. The goo had spilled on the table
and greedy Fatty had licked it all up.

73

Boing!

As the drums in his belly grew louder, Fatty started burping and belching and blowing off like a *mini* windy set of bagpipes. And with each smelly outburst he grew bigger and stranger and scarier.

Burp!

Belch!

Blow Off!

↑
Happy Sally
Monster

The Sally Monster
peered at Fatty through
her pigtails and smiled.
An ordinary cat had
frightened her, but now
that Fatty was all misshapen and
monsterish she really liked him.

They immediately started playing
together, and when I say playing I
mean charging around the living room,
jumping all over the furniture and
making as much mess as it's possible
for a monster
babysitter and
a monster cat
to do.

my
Beanbag!

I kept my back to the wall because I
didn't want to get in their way and
end up squashed into the carpet. But
eventually they wore each other out
and collapsed on to the sofa, their
burps and belches soon replaced with
loud rumbling snores.

My mouth fell open when I looked around at all the mess. It was like a herd of angry elephants had stampeded through the room. Then I heard another frightening sound, but it wasn't the *boing, boing, boing* of a distant bongo drum, it was something much, much scarier.

It was the *jingle jangle* of keys in the front door.

GULP!

Mum and Dad came in — and
stopped abruptly. They looked at me,
they looked at the room, and then they
looked back at me again. Mum opened
and closed her mouth a few times but
nothing came out. It was as though she
couldn't quite find the words.

Dad sloping away ←

Eventually she *did* find the words and shrieked them at the top of her voice: 'WHAT ON EARTH HAPPENED IN HERE?'

Dad quickly sloped away because that's what he usually does when Mum raises her voice.

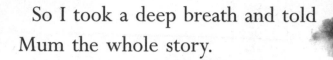

So I took a deep breath and told
Mum the whole story.

When I finished Mum didn't say
anything. I think she needed a moment
to take it all in. Then she wandered
casually over to the sofa.

'These monsters here?' she said in a
calm level tone.

I looked over and saw Sally fast
asleep on the sofa with Fatty curled up
peacefully on her lap. They were not

big or burping or monsterish at all.

In fact they looked just like a regular babysitter and a regular cat taking a pleasant nap.

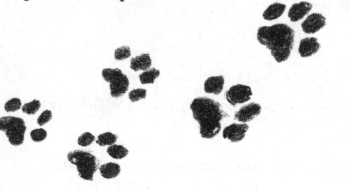

'But . . .' I said feebly.

'I suspect there's only one LITTLE MONSTER in this room,' Mum said sternly. 'And that LITTLE MONSTER is going to have a lot of tidying up to do in the morning.'

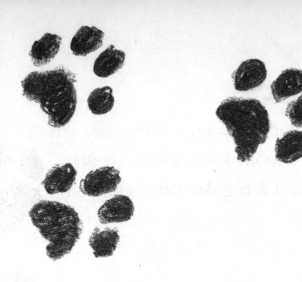

As usual there was no point
in arguing because no one would ever
believe me.

Sally woke up a moment later and
even she couldn't remember what
really happened. *And* she had the cheek
to be cross with me for flushing her
science project down the loo.

Sally collected her books from the
table and frowned at the sticky brown
paw prints all over the pages – sticky

brown paw prints that mysteriously got
bigger and bigger. Then she peered
inside her notebook at the completed
recipe for Runny Chocolate and a tiny
smile flickered across her face.

So maybe I've not seen
the last of the Sally
Monster!

JC

Jake Cake
Productions

JAKE CAKE
AND THE
Missing
Mummy

School trips are generally OK. You still have to learn stuff because there are workbooks to fill in, but most of it is drawing, which I like doing anyway. And the teachers are in a better mood than usual.

Some of them even
wear trainers instead of
shoes and crack
jokes, which is
kind of
embarrassing. But
nothing is more
embarrassing on a
school trip than being
the child of a parent
who has volunteered
to help for the day.

Scrub

Scrub

'Oh, Angel Cake, you really are a
mucky little monkey!' Mum sighed as
she licked a tissue and
scrubbed it
across my face.

The other kids giggled and whispered
as Mum weaved her way back to the
front of the bus, while I stared at my
shoes and prayed for the ground to
swallow me whole.

Before we left
home Mum
had given me
a lecture
about
behaving
myself
and not
making up
stories about
dive-bombing bats or
any other nonsense.

(On the last school trip to the local caves I got into a huge amount of trouble with an army of giant bats — but I'll tell you about that another time.) This time we were going to a museum to see things from ancient Egypt so I wasn't too worried. How much trouble could I get into in a dusty old museum?

The museum was huge and as my class snaked its way through the different rooms I trailed along right at the back and hoped Mum would ignore me. My plan was working very well until I lingered too long over a glass case with a boy mummy inside and got left behind.

The label said the boy mummy
had been the same age as me,
which was hard to believe
     because he was only half my
     size. My workbook said
          people were much smaller
          in those days but I think
          being made into a mummy
          had more to do with it.

Before they wrap you up in bandages
they do lots of things to make you
shrivel up like a prune.

I was just wondering how
crinkly the mummy
was under his
bandages when a
terrifying sound
echoed through the
whole building. I
nearly leapt out of
my skin.

me wondering

'ANGEL CAKE! YOU'RE AS
SLOW AS A SLUGGISH SNAIL!'
Mum shrieked. 'WILL YOU PLEASE
REJOIN THE GROUP
IMMEDIATELY!'

With my face glowing as
red as a tomato I hurried
to catch them up.

me red as
a tomato

The whole class had
gathered around a big
lump of yellow stone with squiggly
lines and
pictures on it.

Our history teacher Mrs Marsh was
telling the class that the squiggles and
pictures were actually ancient
Egyptian writing called hieroglyphics,
and if we turned to page six in
our workbooks . . .

GULP!

I frantically rummaged
through my bag but the
workbook wasn't there.
I would definitely
be in trouble if I
owned up to
losing it.

GULP!

Mum would start sighing and talking at the top of her voice again, calling me a Silly Billy or Forgetful Elephant or something embarrassing like that. I already had *two* Angel Cakes to live down and I couldn't risk any more.

There was nothing else for it, I HAD to find my workbook!

Mum was busy talking to the other teachers using their first names (she called Mr Jenson 'Bob' and she called Mrs Marsh 'Mary',

which was very strange because you don't like to think of your teachers having proper names). So I sneaked back the way I'd come, searching the floor for my workbook. Eventually I saw it next to the mummy case where Mum had made me jump. I picked it up, heaving a sigh of relief, and then I noticed something odd.

The glass case that *had* contained the boy mummy was empty!

I went round the side of the case. The lid was slightly open and there were pale dusty footprints zigzagging away from it on the shiny marble floor!

GULP!

Looking around I saw a few people wandering through the displays. But none of them was small and thin and wrapped in bandages. And none of them was screaming, so they probably hadn't seen the mummy either.

There was a mummy on the loose!

I had two choices: I could either sneak back to my group with my

workbook and stay out of trouble, or
I could follow the footprints and risk
getting into tons of trouble.

Hmmm . . .

Shoving my workbook in my
rucksack, I set about
tracking the trail of
dusty footprints.

I hadn't gone far when
I found a strip of
bandage. I picked it up
and carried on a little
further — and found

another, and another, and another.

You'd think people might wonder why
a kid was wandering around the
museum on his own with what quickly
became a big bundle of dirty cloth, but
they were much too busy peering into
glass cases and studying guidebooks to
even notice.

After tracking the footsteps through the whole museum they suddenly stopped outside a small door in one of the giant hallways. As I picked up the last scrap of bandage, it suddenly dawned on me that the mummy probably wasn't covered up any more. My hand hovered over the door handle while I decided if I still wanted to know how crinkly a mummy was under its bandages.

But I was more curious than scared, and because I was probably already in trouble I didn't want it to be for nothing, so I took a deep breath and opened the door.

Instead of facing a scary, nudie, mouldy mummy, I was confronted by a load of mops and brooms sticking out of a bucket like a dreary bunch of flowers.

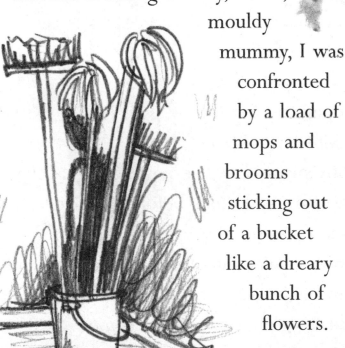

'Hello?' I whispered, poking my head inside.

'Hello,' replied the brooms and mops.

Now I've seen many strange things during my unbelievable  adventures but I've never seen talking brooms and mops before. I looked closer and noticed one of the mops was smaller than the rest and had arms and legs and a head, and a pair of eyes that were peering back at me.

'Are you the mummy?' I gasped, realizing it was a bit of a silly question.

'Er, yes, I suppose I am,' said the mummy. (You might be wondering why the mummy was speaking English and not ancient Egyptian. I did too but decided he'd probably picked it up from all the people who passed through the museum to gawp at him.)

'Someone woke me up,' said the mummy. 'Someone with a very loud voice.'

'That was my mum,' I sighed.

'Your mummy?' said the mummy.

'Yes, my mummy, well, my mum, but she's not *a* mummy.'

'Your mummy's not a mummy?'

I nodded uncertainly. I was beginning to confuse myself when a horrific sound thundered through the museum. I froze to the spot and felt my blood run cold.

'JAKE CAKE, WHAT ON EARTH DO YOU THINK YOU'RE DOING?'

'That's my mum,' I gulped.

'Oh,' said the mummy, in a way that suggested his own mum had a similar angry voice that made camels stampede into the Nile (which my workbook says is a famous river in Egypt).

Mum marched down the hallway and stood over me with her arms folded. 'I assume you have a good explanation for wandering off on your own?' she said, tapping her foot impatiently on the marble floor.

'I lost my workbook where the mummy was, but when I went back it wasn't there any more,' I blurted out.

Mum reached over my head and plucked the workbook from my rucksack. 'This workbook wasn't there?' she said, eyeing me suspiciously.

'Yes! I mean no! I mean the workbook *was* there but the *mummy* was gone! So I followed the dusty footprints and tracked it here inside the broom cupboard.' I held up the pile of dirty bandages as proof. 'Look, these are his clothes!'

Mum snatched the bandages from me and threw them into the cupboard. 'The janitor will be very cross if he finds you playing "mummies" with his cleaning rags . . .'

I won't bore you with the rest of what Mum said because it would just be a big long rant about 'making up stories' and 'noses growing long'.

Mum led me back to the group and sat me down at the back.

All the other kids were asking Mrs Marsh questions about ancient Egypt and I decided the best plan would be to keep quiet. That was until a small brown head poked out through the top of my rucksack and said, 'Sorry I got you into trouble with your mummy.'

I gasped and quickly shoved it back inside. There was a mummy in my rucksack – and all I could think about was how much more trouble I would be in if Mum caught me with one of the ancient Egyptian exhibits!

'It's not your fault,' I whispered. 'I always get into trouble anyway, but you must go back before someone notices you're missing or we'll both be in more trouble than we can handle.'

'I can't go back without Phelix. He's meant to be with me but someone has moved him,' said the mummy. He sounded quite upset. 'That's why I got out in the first place, so I could find him and get him back.'

'Who's Phelix?' I asked.

'He's my cat,' said the mummy. 'I can't go back to sleep without him.'

'But the museum's huge!' I said. 'How will you find him before someone notices you're missing?'

'JAKE CAKE!' snapped Mrs Marsh from the other side of the room. 'Am I to understand from your mumbling that you have something fascinating to share with us about the ancient Egyptians?'

GULP!

Looking around I could see everyone had been watching me talking to my rucksack. Mrs Marsh fixed me with a stare

Mrs March Staring

that said she was
waiting for an
answer, and the look
on Mum's face told
me that it had better
be a good one.

mum's
Stare

'Er . . .' I said.

'Come along!' demanded Mrs
Marsh. 'Stand up and share your
thoughts with the class. I'm sure
we're all very keen to know what
unique insights you've gleaned from
your own private little tour.'

I stood up awkwardly and stared
around the room, looking for
something to say about ancient
Egyptians, when suddenly I had an idea.

'Excuse me, Mrs Marsh,' I said. 'I was just wondering if we could go and see the cat mummies?'

There were giggles from the other kids and Mum looked very disappointed because I'd said something so silly, but Mrs Marsh seemed pleasantly surprised.

'Quiet, everyone,' she said, waving
her arms in the air. 'Jake has just raised
a very interesting historical fact. The
ancient Egyptians *were indeed* buried
with their pets,

and if you'd studied your workbooks as
Jake obviously has, you would also
know they were particularly fond of
cats.'

I sat back down and tried not to grin.

'Now there is only time to see one
more collection before we need to
catch the bus,' said Mrs Marsh. 'So
who would like to follow Jake's
excellent suggestion and visit the room
of mummified pets?'

Suddenly everyone's hand went up in the air, including Mum's, until she realized where she was and quickly put it back down again. Even the mummy's bony hand shot out of my rucksack and I let out a quick yelp before shoving it back inside.

'Then it's decided,' said Mrs Marsh. 'Everyone follow me.'

The room of mummified pets was very big and most of the small mummies were roughly cat-shaped.

If I was looking for *my* cat among the mummies it would be easy because Fatty would be the only one shaped like a football, but

FATTY MUMMY

finding Phelix would be difficult because all of these looked the same and there were loads and loads of them.

'There he is!' said an excited voice from inside my bag and a bony finger popped out and wiggled at a large display case.

'Which one?' I whispered. 'They all look the same.'

'The one with the missing ear,' said the mummy. 'That's my Phelix.'

Phelix
(very cute)

I could see Phelix in the middle of
a dozen other cat mummies who
all had two ears but weren't as
cute. 'How are we supposed
to get him out with everyone
watching?' I said, and it slowly
dawned on me that I was probably
about to get in trouble again.

'If you put me down I can get
him out, but you need to cause a
diversion,' said the mummy.

As I put my rucksack down on
the floor a hand landed on my
head and started ruffling my hair.

'Who's my clever little Angel
Cake?' Mum said, smiling proudly.

'I am?' I said helplessly. Helpless
because the other kids were sniggering
again at the name Angel Cake (which I
would definitely never live down),

and helpless because I knew I would
have to ruin all my good work by
causing a diversion.

Now if I'd had time to think about it,
I probably could have come up with
something clever. Something that
would have kept me out of trouble and
saved any further humiliation. But I
didn't have time for
that, so I pointed
across the room
and screamed
at the
top of
my voice.

'AAAARRRRRRRGH! THERE'S
AN ESCAPED MUMMY!'

All the other kids suddenly started
screaming and running
around in a panic.

Mr Jenson, Mrs Marsh and Mum ran after them, flapping their hands in the air as they tried to control the terrified mob.

The room of mummified pets was in chaos, and in all the confusion the mummy snatched Phelix from the display case and jumped back in my rucksack without being seen.

PHEW!

When everything calmed down Mum was too angry to speak. She just grabbed my arm and marched me through the museum. But I still had one thing left to do.

As we passed by the mummy case I
dropped my bag
beside it without
Mum seeing.

'Ouch!' yelped the bag. Mum thought it was me, moaning about being tugged  along by the arm, so she tugged a bit harder. When we got outside I stopped suddenly and Mum nearly yanked my arm off.

'Oh no!' I said, in my best 'acting surprised' voice. 'I've lost my rucksack.'

I'm not completely sure what Mum
was saying as we made our way back
through the museum. She was talking
through gritted teeth and was growling
quite a lot, but no matter how much
trouble I was in it was definitely worth
it. Grabbing my bag, I looked inside
the glass case and saw a hastily
rewrapped mummy holding a cat
with one ear in his arms.
There was a faint
smile on his
bandaged face
and as I moved
away his hand
gave the smallest
wave.

Tiny
wave

The escaped mummy was all anyone spoke about for a whole week at school, and it took even longer to get back into Mum's good books. On the plus side I didn't get called Angel Cake for a very long time afterwards because Mum said, 'Angels don't behave like THAT!'

She also refused to volunteer for
a school trip ever again, explaining it
was far too embarrassing.

And for once, I have to say, I
definitely agree with my mummy!

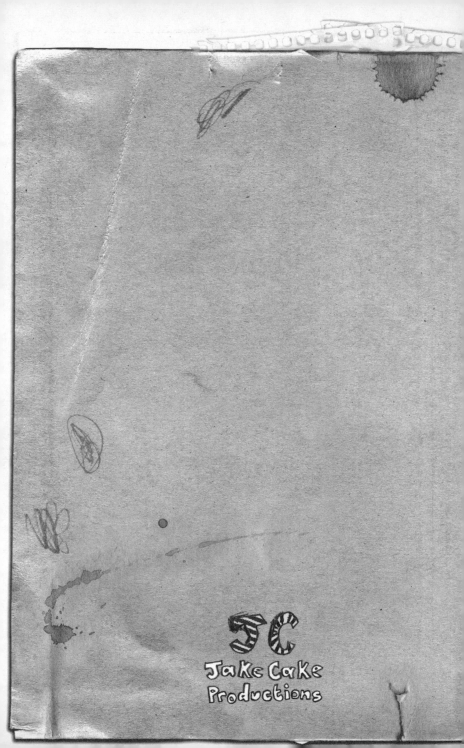

JC

Jake Cake
Productions

NAME: Werewolf teacher (Mrs Beady)

AGE: I think Mrs Beady is quite old

WEIGHT: I wonder if the Werewolf tea→cher and Mrs Beady weigh the same?

How To Spot One: a Werewolf is bigger than a dog and they go "Ooooowww!" all the time.

Comments: Werewolves are a bit of a handful - but they're lots of fun. And they're a lot more fun than Maths!

OOOOoooowww!

JC
Jake Cake
Productions

UNBELIEVABLE ADVENTURE REPORT

NAME: Monster Babysitter (Sally)

AGE: I think she's about 16 years old

WEIGHT: not very much when she's Sally - but LOADS more when she's a MONSTER!

How To Spot One: Listen for the distant sound of bongo drums and the smell of rotten SPROUTS!

Comments: Sally still has the formula for RUNNY CHOCOLATE so if you ever have a babysitter called Sally - you'd better **WATCH OUT!** cos

She'll ~~break~~ TRASH the house and you'll get into LOADS of TROUBLE!

Jake Cake Productions

UNBELIEVABLE ADVENTURE REPORT

OFFICIAL JC DOCUMENT

NAME: Mummy (not the "mum" kind.)

AGE: THOUSANDS of years old!!!

WEIGHT: not very much cos they're very Dusty!

How To Spot One: Go to a MUSEUM - one that has stuff from EGYPT.

Comments: the mummy I met was very friendly but there are probably scary ones too - ones that run after you waving their arms and going "Arrrggghhh!"

JC
Jake Cake
Productions

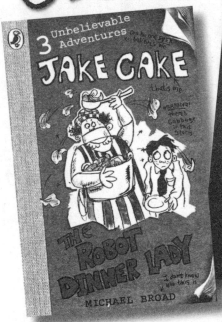
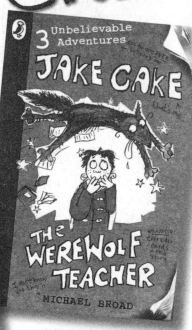